BACKSTREET BOYS

backstage pass

Now and forever!

millennium
Scrapbook

SCHOLASTIC INC.

NEW YORK TORONTO LONDON AUCKLAND SYDNEY
MEXICO CITY NEW DELHI HONG KONG

Photography Credits

ISBN 0-439-14975-4

12 11 10 9 8 7 6 5 4 3 2 1   9/9 0 1 2 3 4/0

Printed in the U.S.A.
First Scholastic printing, October 1999

WHAT'S INSIDE

Nick croons a ballad just for you!

The Boys Are Here Now and Forever!!

BACK IN THE EARLY '90'S, if you uttered the words, "Backstreet Boys" you probably would have been faced with blank stares, or greeted with the response, "Backstreet WHO?" Okay, fast forward a few years — their debut album, *Backstreet Boys,* sold over 10 million copies! And then *everyone* knew who they were. True — but they still got zippo respect. "They're one hit wonders, they'll never last." That's what everyone said. Check it, *everyone* was wrong, 'cause . . .

BACKSTREET'S BACK — AND THEY'RE BIGGER THAN EVER!!

The year 1999 was the dawn of their smash second album, *Millennium*. It proved beyond a doubt that BSB are "HTS"— Here To Stay! But the road to the top hasn't exactly been smooth — it's been paved with potholes and speed bumps. This amazing scrapbook gives you the inside scoop on the Backstreet Boys' wild ride — it tells all, their heartbreaks, loves, losses, traumas, and triumphs. Learn cool facts. Uncover secrets. And more, more, more!

So what are you waiting for? Turn the page and get up to speed on the most amazing band in the land.

Whoo-hoo!

millennium Madness!

Definition: Sophomore slump. What happens when a band's *first* album does blockbuster biz—and the follow-up totally tanks. [See: Hootie and the Blowfish, Alanis Morissette]

IT COULDA HAPPENED TO THE BACKSTREET BOYS, TOO. Many said it would. But, nuh-*uh*. The May 1999 release of their second album, *Millennium*, sold an astounding 1.3 million copies its first week out (that's right, its first *week*!). That shattered Garth Brooks' over-hyped record of 1.08 million, just set in November 1998. And what makes this sales record even more amazing is that it came during May, a month where record stores don't usually see a lot of business. Garth's album, on the other hand, was sold during the height of the Christmas season.

Needless to say, the Boys made HISTORY, and their album soared to NUMBER ONE, even kicking Ricky Martin out of that coveted position! By its fourth week of release, *Millennium* had reaped sales of over five million copies, and firmly secured the number one spot for weeks.

How'd They Do It?

True, the Boys have tons and tons of teen fans who rushed to the stores to scoop up their long-awaited release. But lots of adults snapped it up, too. (Two songs from their last album, "Quit Playing Games (With My Heart)" and "As Long

As You Love Me" were big hits on adult contemporary stations.) Since adults liked what they heard last time, it was a no-brainer to snare the new one.

WE ♥ MTV — that's what the band should be saying — the music video channel was on the hype-tip, practically 24–7. Starting two days before *Millennium*'s release, the Boys appeared practically nonstop on the station. An unbelievable 10,000 fans flooded Times Square when BSB appeared live at MTV's studios — MTV's largest street crowd ever!

Brian, Howie, AJ, and Kevin pose with MTV's Carson Daly.

They Say...

Lots has been written about the Backstreet Boys. Used to be, it wasn't complimentary. But the press has changed its tune, once everyone tuned into *Millennium*.

The Boys at a press conference for the launch of Millennium.

Before, they'd been dissed as "prefab, too pretty, too perfectly choreographed." But look at what they're saying now:

"...The ballad 'Show Me the Meaning of Being Lonely' digs its melodic claws into your skull on the first listen — it's the swooniest blending of the five vocalists' timbres to date, and mighty pretty besides."

– Rolling Stone*, June 10, 1999*

"The second U.S. release from leading boy band Backstreet Boys might as well be deemed a smash, even before its release. ...The album is as deep as the ocean blue, with richly produced singles that extend the vocal prowess of each of the group's members...while maintaining the essential BSB sound that will send fans swooning into a vaporous faint all over again."

– Billboard*, May 29, 1999*

What the Boys Are Saying

Of course, the band was way psyched that *Millennium* was such a mega hit. Hard to imagine, then, that there was a lot of doubt as to whether or not there would even *be* a second album. Doubt in everyone's mind except the Backstreet Boys, that is. As Howie D. told MTV News'

John Norris recently, "I don't think we were ever at a point where there would be no other Backstreet record. . . . We went through a lot of stuff . . . last year. With Brian's heart surgery; I had a sister that passed away . . . We had a lot of business issues that had to get solved." Later, at a press conference, Howie called the record, "our strongest . . . We feel the lyrical content, the musical quality, the message within the lyrics is a positive step."

With all their "problems" behind them, the Boys were poised for success. Yet, they really didn't care about the sales — their hearts were with the music. "We're not really looking at sales," Kevin told *Reuters*. "If you make good music and keep trying to outdo your last album as far as quality of music, the sales will come."

The Boys show off their slick dance moves on stage.

And how do they feel about critics? ". . . we're not trying to please the critics, we're trying to please ourselves and our fans," Howie D. told *Jam!Music*.

What the Boys Are Singing — Three **Millennium** Songs

The track "Larger than Life" is dedicated to their fans. "It's almost like a thank-you song for all they've done. They're there for us through all our ups and downs," Howie said in an online chat.

"The Perfect Fan" is about Brian's mother. It is one of two songs on the album that members of the BSB, who traditionally work with outside writers, co-wrote. (Brian got credit for that one.) The other song is the piano-laden ballad "Back to Your Heart" credited partly to Kevin.

bsb-the Ups and downs

The Backstreet Boys' career looks a lot like the paths of shooting stars — lots of ups and down. Fasten your seatbelt, let's take a ride:

Nick checked out a BSB article in a magazine.

UP

The Backstreet Boys' tale began in Orlando, Florida, in 1993. It was there that A.J. McLean, Howie Dorough, and Nick Carter kept bumping into each other at various auditions. They formed a singing group in the style of their favorite groups Boyz II Men and Color Me Badd. The trio then added Kevin Richardson (who was working as a Disney World tour guide). But a fifth voice was needed. Enter Brian Littrell (who happened to be Kevin's cousin). And, snap! The Backstreet Boys were formed — under the management of a man named Lou Pearlman (we'll hear more about him later). The Boys were set and ready to make it big.

DOWN

Thud. Their dreams of stardom crashed. Their first single, "We've Got It Goin' On" tanked at number sixty-nine on the charts. The Boys definitely were *not* a big hit on American soil!

A take from one of their earliest shoots, circa 1997.

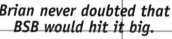

Brian never doubted that BSB would hit it big.

UP

So, Mr. Pearlman recruited a man who might help — former New Kids on the Block road manager Johnny Wright, who immediately sent BSB packing to Europe. The strategy worked. The Boys became a HUGE hit in Germany, with the rest of Europe soon following. They toured (and soared) through Europe for the next two years, releasing one hit song after another, selling out concerts, and collecting fans by the millions.

Nick sneaks in some pool time.

DOWN

Surely, American fans would have gotten wind
of this boy band sensation by now, but nuh-*uh*!
Each time they'd try to get airplay on U.S. radio
stations, they were turned away. BSB needed
another year abroad before the time was right
to reach success in their homeland.

UP

In 1994, finally American fans were ready for
the Boys! After three years of touring over-
seas, they returned to the U.S. and their single "Quit Playing Games (With My Heart)"
topped the charts at NUMBER ONE!

DOWN

Happy? Well, *yeah*! Feeling compensated? Not. Four singles
and $200 million in sales later, the Boys had a falling out
with their manager. They believed they weren't getting their
fair share of the profits. "The contracts weren't fair," Kevin com-
plained to *Rolling Stone*. "And we were kept on the road, and before
you know it, two or three years and millions of dollars go by."
To add insult to injury, the Boys discovered that 'N Sync, their
main competition in the pop market, were managed by none other
than Lou Pearlman! "That hurt our feelings," Kevin admitted to *Rolling
Stone*. "Because for a while it was like, 'We're a family.' Then all of a
sudden, 'It's business, guys, sorry.' We have nothing against . . . that
group, personally. It was [Pearlman's] not being honest."

UP

Eventually, the Boys reached an agreement with Mr. Pearlman (though the terms are top secret), and signed with a new, L.A.-based team of managers — a new beginning, in a sense.

Kevin and A.J. slip on their shades as the Boys pose for the camera at the 1997 Billboard Awards.

DOWN

In 1998, the business side was finally ironed out; tragically, the personal lives of two of the guys went into a heart-wrenching tailspin. Brian had to endure heart surgery. Howie's sister, Caroline, died. Kevin and Brian's grandfather also passed away during that year.

"We weren't happy," A.J. told *Jam!Music*. "We were getting up on stage every night and, me personally, I felt like I was getting up on stage just because I had to."

The Boys always have time to get together for a photo op!

Lookin' cool at a press conference at the All Star Café in New York City.

UP, UP, UP MILLENNIUM!!

"We've worked very hard on this new album and hope that people enjoy the music as much as they have in the past," Howie said in an online chat. "It's not that we tried to be a more mature Backstreet Boys. We were just trying to set new goals and challenge ourselves musically." Mission *totally* accomplished. And zillions of fans *totally* got it. *Millennium* is the icing on a cake that — as you now see — has *many* layers. How sweet 'n' tasty it is!

REWIND:
your backstory

Fill in Your Own Backstreet Boys Memories

How I First Heard About the Backstreet Boys:

How Old I Was:

Where I First Saw the Backstreet Boys (on TV, in concert):

My First Reaction to "Quit Playing Games (With My Heart)":

The BSB I was most into:

My Favorite BSB song from Millennium:

Paste Your First **Favorite** BSB Picture Here

Chapter Three

Kevin richardson:
the boys' big brother

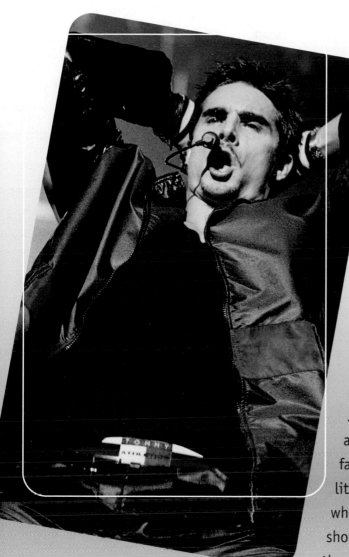

He may not be the flashiest dancer, and he may

not get the biggest parts to sing. But Kevin Richardson is the one who really keeps the rest of the Boys on track. He approaches each task he's given with a real "take charge" attitude. At twenty-seven, Kevin is the oldest member of the group. He's sort of like the band's big brother. "These guys are like family," Kevin told *Teen* magazine. "We've been together for six years, and we've gone through a lot together. It sounds kind of corny, but we fight like brothers and we love each other like brothers."

Kevin grew up on a ten acre farm in Harrisburg, Kentucky, where his family raised their own cows and pigs. Kevin's mom, Ann, told *Rolling Stone* that her son caught the performance bug early at a camp run by his father. "He began to do little skits and sing when the camp had its show-time nights, and the girls would start hollering." That was a good predictor of Kev's future!

Kevin also loved singing in his church's choir. And when he graduated from high school, he played keyboards and sang in a band called Paradise. One day, Kevin's father suggested that he check out the entertainment scene in Orlando. Kevin took Dad's advice, and got a job as a tour guide. That's where he hooked up with A.J., Nick, and Howie.

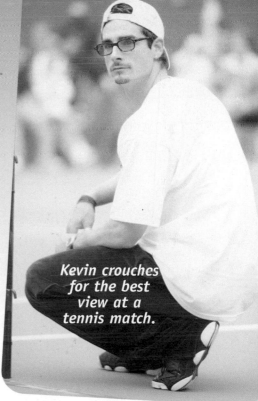

Kevin crouches for the best view at a tennis match.

A Boy in a hood!

But then, tragedy struck. Kevin was living in Orlando when his dad was diagnosed with colon cancer. When Kev found out that his father was sick, he moved back home to Kentucky. Sadly, Mr. Richardson soon passed away. Kevin stuck close to home for almost a year before returning to Orlando. When he did rejoin the Backstreet Boys, it was with a new outlook. "I want to live my life in a way that would make him [Dad] proud. I think he'd be pleased that I worked at the band. As long as I do what makes me happy, without sacrificing my morals, and follow what I was brought up to believe, he'll be proud." — *Top of the Pops*

Kevin's Confession

It's no shock that classically handsome Kevin has done some modeling, and when he and the rest of the band got a call from designer Donatella Versace to attend her fashion show in Milan, Italy, Kevin couldn't get there fast enough! Amazingly, he actually ended up walking down the runway as a model! "That night at dinner, I'm sitting next to Naomi Campbell, with Donatella on the other side of me," he gushed to Rolling Stone. Even better, the next night was his birthday. Kate Moss sang to him and Donatella surprised him with a cake!

Yes, Kevin has a girlfriend.
In fact, he's been dating
her for seven years!

Vital Stats

Full Name: Kevin Scott Richardson

Birth Date: October 3, 1972

Zodiac Sign: Libra

Birth Place: Lexington, Kentucky

Height: 6'1"

Hair: Dark brown

Eyes: Hazel

Parents: Ann and Jerald Richardson Sr.

Sibs: Brothers Jerald and Tim

Pet: A cat named Quincy

BROW-BOY:

"I wouldn't let anybody touch my eyebrows because I don't want to look like a madeup girl or whatever. They're big ol' Groucho Marx brows. I think you just have to be happy with what God gives you."

brian littrell:
b-rok

Nah, Nick isn't really trying to choke Brian — the Boys are as close as brothers!

Twenty-four-year-old Brian Littrell, or B-Rok, as the other Boys sometimes call him, spent his early years in Lexington, Kentucky, singing in his local church, and other regional houses of worship, at revivals, and even weddings. Religious much? You bet.

Brian feels he has a lot to thank God for. As a young child he was very ill — and didn't even know it. "I was born with a heart murmur," he told *BOP*. "I have a hole in my heart and the doctors didn't know."

It wasn't until 1980, when Brian cracked his head on the sidewalk and was rushed to the hospital, that his parents found out that their boy was seriously ill. At the hospital, complications set in and Brian got a blood infection. He recounts the trauma. "I had no chance of living whatsoever. The doctors were

telling my mother and father to go ahead and make funeral arrangements."

But then the unexpected happened — Brian surprised everyone and recovered! He still wasn't completely healed, though.

In May 1998, Brian underwent heart surgery. "I delayed surgery twice because of the tours," Brian told *Rolling Stone*. "I mean, the saddest thing is that I scheduled open-heart surgery around my work schedule. It was like nobody really cared or felt that it was important, because the career was moving on." Thankfully, Brian had the surgery and pulled through just fine. Like the Backstreet Boys, Brian's back and better than ever.

What's up?

Brian's Confession

He sometimes uses his dog as a diversionary tactic. "I'll have someone hold him up and be like, 'Look, everybody. Look at the cute puppy!' Then I can slip by fans unnoticed."

On the *Girlfriend* Front

Yes, Brian has a girlfriend. Her name's Leighanne Wallace and she's an actress and lives on the West Coast.

Vital Stats

Full Name: Brian Thomas Littrell

Birth Date: February 20, 1975

Zodiac Sign: Pisces

Birth Place: Lexington, Kentucky

Height: 5'7"

Hair: Dirty blond

Eyes: Blue

Parents: Jackie and Harold Littrell

Sibs: Older brother Harold

Pet: A tiny Chihuahua named Little Tyke

Fact *or Fiction?*

When Leighanne makes her next movie, *Olive Juice*, Brian might have a cameo.

INSIGHTFUL QUOTE:

"Music is my love, but it's my job. There's things that used to be taken for granted that aren't now: time with your family, time to enjoy the fruits of your labor."
– Rolling Stone

Chapter Five
Cutie Cousins

Not only are Kevin and Brian first cousins — Kevin's mom, Ann, and Brian's dad, Harold, are sister and brother — they know A LOT about each other! Check it out:

★ Kevin remembers going to Brian's house to play "Star Wars" when he was a child. Kevin was always Darth Vader and Harold (Brian's brother) was always Luke Skywalker. But they never wanted Brian to play, 'cause he was too young. POOR BRIAN!

★ Kevin likes the relaxed way in which Brian approaches things, but sometimes he feels that Brian is just *too* relaxed!

★ Kevin's favorite toy was his BMX bike. He thought he was just the coolest when he rode it around!

★ Brian remembers playing with his toy soldiers on the volleyball court at Kevin's dad's house.

★ Brian loved it when Kevin played the piano, and he always wished he'd learned to play the way Kevin did.

★ Brian thinks that he and Kevin grew up almost like brothers, but he can talk to Kevin about things he might not tell his brother.

★ *Most of all, both Boys always have and always will trust each other. That's the coolest thing of all.*

Backstreet Boys

a.j. mclean:
the rebel

Cool hat, A.J.!

Twenty-one-year old A.J. McLean is the rebel of the group.
Multi-tattooed, pierced, and wild-haired, A.J. loves to be recognized, and gets a real kick out of going on the band's Web sites to talk to fans.

A.J. is, and always has been, a ham. His very first acting job was when he was seven years old. He played Dopey in *Snow White and the Seven Dwarfs*, and stole the show! "I was the main squeeze," A.J. told a *Scholastic* writer. "All the girls thought I was really cute. And I went out and signed autographs for all the little kids. And it was funny — back then I signed my full name, because that's what I thought you were supposed to do. But now, I just write, 'A.J.' because that's who I am."

By the time A.J. was in sixth grade, he had appeared in twenty-seven productions. And in junior high, he won a part on the Nickelodeon TV Show *Hi Honey, I'm Home*. A.J. took classes in dancing, singing, and acting — he knew what he wanted to do. It all clicked when he met up with Nick and Howie.

Carefree A.J. might *seem* like he's just into having a good time, but he's had to confront some real issues in

his life. When he was just four years old, his dad left. He didn't hear from him until two years ago when A.J. spotted his dad's return address on a child-support notice. A.J. drove out to his dad's place and just knocked on the door. When his dad opened the door, the two embraced, crying. Then A.J. noticed that his dad had all this Backstreet Boys stuff hanging on his walls. A.J. couldn't believe that his dad had been following the Boys all this time, yet never tried to make contact with him.

Vital Stats

Full Name: Alexander James McLean

Birth Date: January 9, 1978

Zodiac Sign: Capricorn

Birth Place: West Palm Beach, Florida

Height: 5'9"

Hair: Brown

Eyes: Brown

Parents: Denise and Bob McLean (his parents were divorced when he was four years old)

Sibs: None

Pet: A dachshund named Tobi Wan Kenobi (*that's* pretty funny!)

Since the emotional reunion, things have calmed down a bit — though the sitch is still far from ideal. "He remarried, and his wife is pushing him down my throat," A.J. told *Rolling Stone*. "If he would do things in moderation, maybe we could get a father-son relationship back. But being so pushy, I don't want to do it."

On the Girlfriend Front

Yes, A.J. has a girlfriend. She's an aspiring singer.

HONEST QUOTE:

"I'm the complete opposite of every clean-cut, decent-looking guy you could think of, yet I have the biggest heart in the world." – *Teen*

howie dorough:
a real sweetie

Twenty-six-year-old Howie Dorough, or Howie D., is known to others as Sweet D. "Once, when we couldn't sign autographs because there were too many fans, he was too nice and stopped — and got trampled by them," A.J. told *Teen People*.

Son of a Puerto Rican mom and an Irish dad, Howie has been performing since he was six. At the ripe old age of seven, he nabbed the role of a Lollipop Guild Munchkin in his first-grade play, *The Wizard of Oz*. That was the beginning — Howie soon got into the fast-track showbiz whirl. He performed in Orlando community theater productions, appeared in a Nickelodeon TV show called *Welcome Freshman*, and acted in the films *Parenthood* and *Cop and a Half*.

Howie knew that showbiz was going to be his life and at college earned an Associate of Arts degree in music. No wonder many consider him the backbone of BSB.

Unlike the rest of his bandmates, Howie still lives at home. "I come from a large family of five kids. We're all really tight. I used to have an apartment with Kevin and Brian, but I always ended up at my parent's house anyway," he told *Teen*.

Needless to say, Howie was devastated when his sister, Caroline Cochran, died unexpectedly at the age of 37. Everyone was heartbroken when Caroline lost her battle with lupus, a disease that affects the immune system.

Being a Backstreet Boy is his life. "The best thing about being a BSB is getting a chance to travel around the world, see different countries, and meet people every day and make people happy with our music," he said in an online chat.

DID YOU KNOW?

* Howie still tries to live a normal life. "I still go to the grocery store," he told *Teen*. "I go to the malls. It's very flattering when people come up and ask me for an autograph."
* Howie loves Oreo Cookies and Cream ice cream.
* Howie's favorite subject in school was math.

Howie's Confession

"I love performing. That's where I'm most comfortable. I'm usually a little bit nervous right before I go on, especially if I make a mistake at the beginning of the show." —Teen

Vital Stats

Full Name: Howard Dwaine Dorough

Birth Date: August 22, 1973

Zodiac Sign: Leo

Birth Place: Orlando, Florida

Height: 5'6"

Hair: Brown

Eyes: Brown

Parents: Paula and Hoke Dorough

Sibs: Brother John; Sisters Polly, Caroline (passed away), and Angela

Chapter Eight

Nick Carter:
Shy heartthrob

Is that smile for real?

From the time he was a toddler, Nick was an entertainer. His family gladly tells tales of their baby boy, wearing only diapers, bustin' a move on the dance floor of a club his grandfather owned.

In the fourth grade, the showbiz bug bit when Nick landed the lead in a local production of *Phantom of the Opera*. He entered lots of talent shows, and remembers one in which he tried an impersonation of Elvis — leg shake and all! "I had to try," he told *Live & Kicking* magazine. "I'm not really a dancer though. You gotta remember, I was really young when I started doing that stuff."

But he was doing *something* right and was soon the featured vocalist at the Tampa Bay Buccaneers pre-game shows. This NFL gig lasted two years, and then when Nick was twelve, he won top prize on the 1992 *New Original Amateur Hour* TV show. Local commercial gigs came quickly after that, and Nick kept busy performing and auditioning at Tampa and Orlando events. Even though he was only in junior high

at that time, Nick made friends with two older guys he kept running into at the same gigs — A.J. McLean and Howie Dorough. The three started harmonizing together as a way to pass the time during the long waits at auditions and performances.

Today, of course, nineteen-year-old Nick is a full-fledged member of the Backstreet Boys, and living on his own. But don't try to find Nick's address. He already had to move once because he was tired of being hounded by fans. And boy, do fans run after him! Even though he's the "supposed" heartthrob of the group, Nick is surprisingly shy. "I'm a very quiet person," Nick told *Teen*. "I consider myself a modern-day hermit. I'm happy if I'm in my hotel room just chillin'."

"There's a side of me that nobody knows because I never tell anybody ... In school I was a nerd, I was one of those kids who walked down the hallways always with his head down. I never wanted to get involved in conversation. I wasn't very personable."
— From *The Heart and Soul of Nick Carter* by Jane Carter

Vital Stats

Full Name: Nicholas Gene Carter

Birth Date: January 28, 1980

Zodiac Sign: Aquarius

Birth Place: Jamestown, New York

Height: 6'

Hair: Blond

Eyes: Blue

Parents: Bob and Jane Carter

Sibs: Sister Bobbie Jean (B.J.) and twins Aaron and Angel

Pet: Four pugs

On the **Girlfriend** Front

Yes, Nick has a girlfriend.

DOWN-TO-EARTH QUOTE:

"I don't care if people see me with my hair sticking out to there. It's just me."

Chapter Nine

heartbreaks and Inspirations

THE BOYS HAVE CERTAINLY GONE THROUGH A LOT OF "DOWN" TIMES RECENTLY. Brian's surgery. The loss of Kevin and Brian's grandfather. The passing away of Howie's sister. And the death of producer/songwriter Denniz Pop, who worked on "We've Got It Goin' On" on the first album.

"Denniz was like a second father to us," Nick told journalist Christopher O'Connor. "His music definitely changed what everybody hears nowadays."

In addition, the Boys also experienced a change of management. They're now handled by The Firm, a company that manages rapper Ice Cube among others.

But through all the bad times, there's one *huge* positive note: the Boys have always stuck together. And persevered. A.J. sums it up in *Jam!Music* with these inspiring words: ". . . it was just a huge emotional rollercoaster for all of us. But we had to come together and make a stand for what we wanted as a group. It couldn't be two of us wanted this and three of us wanting that. We came together and said, 'This is what we want to make us happy again.' . . . But now we're back to just getting up on stage and wanting to be there and wanting to perform and wanting to be in the studio, and we're just psyched now. We're happy again."

Backstreet Boys

Chapter Ten

quiz: how Well do You really Know the Backstreet Boys?

How much do you **really** know about Kevin, Brian, A.J., Howie, and Nick? Fill in the blank with the name of the correct BSB. Then check your answers (upside down) at the bottom of the page.

1. Who played Dopey in *Snow White and the Seven Dwarfs?*

2. _____ is afraid of heights.

3. Who once sang in a band called Paradise?

4. _____ is just wild about video games!

5. What is the name of the group's current management?

6. Who is the song "The Perfect Fan" about?

7. Which song on *Millennium* did Kevin co-write?

8. Which BSB still lives at home?

9. Who has a Chihuahua named Little Tyke?

10. _____ loves to draw cartoons.

11. _____ is a qualified ballroom dance instructor.

12. Who admitted he was a nerd in school?

13. _____ played a Lollipop Guild Munchkin in *The Wizard of Oz*.

14. Who has a Beanie Baby collection?

15. _____ spent eight years of his life living in a log cabin.

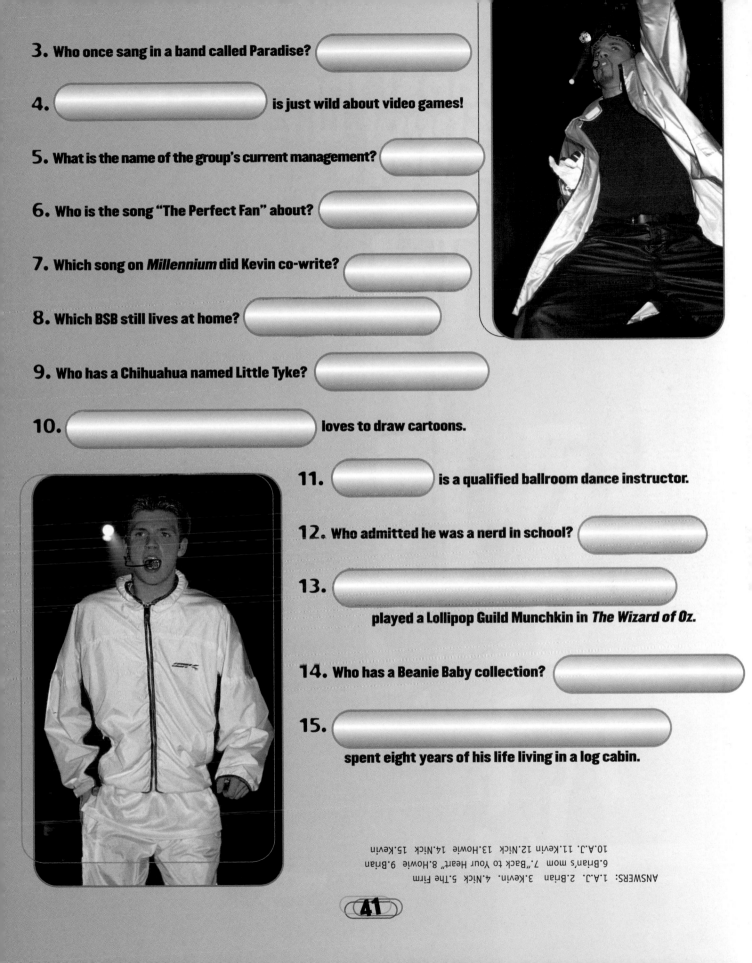

hoops! there it is— a shoot with the boys

BSB TOOK ON NEW YORK CITY in *Backstreet Boys in Concert,* which aired on the Disney Channel. Kevin went horseback riding in Central Park, A.J. and Howie shopped till they dropped in Soho, and, as shown here, Brian and Nick shot hoops in Greenwich Village.

Backstreet Boys in Concert features the group's special performance at The New Amsterdam Theater in New York City, including songs from *Millennium*. The special also includes documentary-style footage of the boys talking about their fame, favorite pastimes, and their cool adventures in New York City.

Sweat much?

Watch out, Nick! Brian's figuring out how to drive to the basket!

Brian practices a fancy trick with the b-ball.

Hey — where'd that ball go? C'mon, B-Rok, look alive!

Brian sizes up the hoop
before taking a shot.

Let's go, Nick!
Brian's gonna score!

discography and awards

Backstreet Boys

U.S. Released: August 1997

1. "We've Got It Goin' On"/ 2. "Quit Playing Games (With My Heart)"/ 3. "As Long As You Love Me"/ 4. "All I Have to Give"/ 5. "Anywhere for You"/ 6. "Hey, Mr. DJ (Keep Playin' This Song)"/ 7. "I'll Never Break Your Heart"/ 8. "Darlin'"/ 9. "Get Down (You're the One for Me)"/ 10. "Set Adrift on Memory Bliss"/ 11. "If You Want It to Be Good Girl (Get Yourself a Bad Boy)"

The guys were psyched after nabbing an award at the '98 MTV Music Awards.

Millennium

U.S. Released: May 1999

1. "Larger Than Life"/ 2. "I Want It That Way"/ 3. "Show Me the Meaning of Being Lonely"/ 4. "It's Gotta Be You"/ 5. "I Need You Tonight"/ 6. "Don't Want You Back"/ 7. "Don't Wanna Lose You Now"/ 8. "The One"/ 9. "Back to Your Heart"/ 10. "Spanish Eyes"/ 11. "No One Else Comes Close"/ 12. "The Perfect Fan"

Singles

"Quit Playing Games (With My Heart)"

"As Long As You Love Me"

"Everybody (Backstreet's Back)"

"All I Have to Give"

"I Want It That Way"

 **Awards**

★ The Boys snagged two Blockbuster Entertainment Awards on May 25, 1999. One for Favorite Group (Pop) and the second for Favorite CD (*Backstreet Boys*).

★ On May 1, 1999, they picked up an award for Best Song at Nickelodeon's *Kids' Choice Awards*.

★ The BSB won four awards at the World Music Awards:
World's Best-selling Pop Group
World's Best-selling R&B Group
World's Best-selling Dance Group
World's Best-selling American Group

You can check out all the latest info on the Backstreet Boys by visiting their official Web site:

http://www.backstreetboys.com

to the *Millennium*– and beyond

What lies ahead for the Backstreet Boys? Well, if they stay on their meteoric path then it's success, success, and more success! No question, there *will* be an album number three — no question this time *no one* will be asking, "Can they do it again?" Because Backstreet's back — now and forever.

Where Do the Boys See Themselves in the Future?

"Hopefully going very strong with BSB and...still at the top of the charts," Howie said in an online chat. And Kevin told *Teen,* "Now that we've gotten successful, they [the press] are like, 'Ah, they'll be gone in a year' or 'They won't last.' But I feel like as long as we keep making hit records and nobody...goes crazy, we can make records for as long as we want."